To Levi,
Always remember you.
perfect just the way you are!

♡ Nina Korn

To Gabby, Chris, and Frankie,

may you always love yourself
as much as I love you.

www.mascotbooks.com

Bella Bunny

For more information, please contact:
Mascot Books
620 Herndon Parkway, Suite 320
Herndon, VA 20170
info@mascotbooks.com

Library of Congress Control Number: 2018904583

CPSIA Code: PRT0618A
ISBN-13: 978-1-68401-761-4

Printed in the United States

Bella Bunny

Written by
Nina Koch

Illustrated by
Chiara Civati

This is Bella. Bella loves her school and loves to read. She is wildly
artistic and very brave. She likes climbing trees, catching frogs by the
creek, and is a super bike rider. She loves her big bows, dresses, and her
purple, sparkly high-top sneakers.

Most of all Bella loves to dance. Every day after school, she walks by Miss
Patti's Dance Studio and wishes she could be in class. She watches beautiful
ballerinas, exciting tappers, and impressive jazz dancers jump, twirl, and
shuffle past the big windows.

"Mama, I want to go to dance class," Bella told her mother. Bella could barely contain her excitement when Mama gave her permission.

The night before class, she laid out her best dance outfit and packed her bag with her ballet slippers and tap shoes. Bella was so excited for her class she woke up extra early, put on her best pink bow, her favorite tutu, and of course, her purple high-tops. She was ready to go before Mama was even awake.

Bella looked at herself in her mirror.

"I look fabulous!"

After breakfast, Bella and Mama headed to Miss Patti's Dance Studio.

On the first day of class, as the bunnies were tying their tap shoes, Addie poked Bella in her bunny belly.

"Why are you so fluffy?"

Bella never thought about her fluff before. She always thought she was perfectly fluffy, but now she was not so sure.

"Don't listen to her," her friend Maggie said.

Bella looked at herself in the dance studio mirror. She was fluffier than the other bunnies in class. Suddenly she was not feeling so fabulous.

"Miss Patti, I am not feeling so good. I think I need to go home." The mean bunnies giggled as Bella left the class.

When she got home, Bella ran upstairs and looked in her mirror again. She thought about the other bunnies in her dance class. They were not as fluffy and their tummies were not as round. Even though she looked different, she couldn't understand why the other bunnies made fun of her.

Bella was so sad that she buried her face in her pillow and cried.

That's when Mama came in.

"Bella what's wrong?"
asked Mama.

Bella told her mom about the
mean bunnies in her dance class,
and how Addie poked her belly and
they all laughed.

"I don't like being fluffy, Mama,"
Bella said with a sad sniffle.

Mama sighed. "Oh Bella. Don't
listen to those bunnies. You are
perfect just the way you are."

"Anytime you are feeling down, I want you to look in the mirror and remind yourself of what a beautiful bunny you are on the inside and on the outside."

After Mama left, Bella decided she
was not going to be sad anymore.
She looked in the mirror and said,

"I am Bella. I'm strong and smart,
I love to dance with all my heart,
I am kind and brave and I love to twirl,
Just you wait, I will change the world."

Each day Bella looked in the mirror and said her Bella Beat, and each day she felt more and more fabulous. She felt like herself again.

When it was time for dance class Bella put on her favorite tutu, her sparkly pink bow, and laced up her purple, sparkly high-tops.

As soon as she arrived, she saw Addie and the mean bunnies were in the corner of the room whispering. Maggie ran up to Bella. It felt like ages since they'd seen each other, so Maggie was especially excited to see her friend, and Bella was relieved to see a friendly face.

Addie walked up to Bella and said, "Dance class is not for fluffy bunnies, you should go home."

Bella started to feel not so fabulous again—her eyes burned and her tummy felt queasy. Maggie squeezed Bella's hand and Bella remembered what Mama had said.

Bella stood tall, took a deep breath, and said her Bella Beat to the mean bunnies:

"I am Bella, I'm strong and smart,
I love to dance with all my heart,
I am kind and brave and I love to twirl,
Just you wait, I will change the world!"

Maggie and the other bunnies in the class cheered! Bella was very proud. She stood up to Addie and the mean bunnies. It felt good to be brave.

Addie and the mean bunnies walked away just as Miss Patti was walking into the dance room.

"Ok bunnies, please find your places at the barre."

Bella could not stop smiling.

"My goodness Bella," said Miss Patti. "Your smile is sparkling brighter than the sparkles on your bow! I am so happy you are back in class today."

Bella was happy to be back too.

Addie and the mean bunnies never made fun of Bella again. Bella continued to work hard in her dance classes and practiced at home.

When it came time for the big show, Bella earned the starring role. On the evening of the big performance, Bella was feeling not so fabulous again. Her tummy was queasy and her heart was pounding. Bella was nervous.

"Bella, are you feeling okay?" Miss Patti asked. "You look a bit pale."

Bella shook her head. "No Miss Patti, I am not okay. My tummy is queasy, my heart is thumping, and my head is so sweaty my bow is falling out. I don't think I can dance tonight. You should pick someone else."

Miss Patti took Bella by the hand and led her to a mirror at the dressing table.

"Bella," said Miss Patti, "I chose you for a reason. I see how hard you work in class and how much you love to dance. You have nothing to be nervous about. I know you will be fabulous."

"But what if they laugh at my fluff?" Bella asked through her tears.

"I know the audience will see the same thing I see—
a strong, talented bunny who loves to dance."
Miss Patti gave Bella a little squeeze and walked away.

Bella was left looking at the mirror trying to find the talented, strong, amazing bunny Miss Patti was talking about.

Just then, Bella started to smile. She took a deep breath said her Bella Beat.

"I am Bella. I'm strong and smart,
I love to dance with all my heart,
I am kind and brave and I love to twirl,
Just you wait, I will change the world!"

Bella's heart stopped pounding, her tummy did not feel queasy. She felt brave and strong.

She took her place on stage, the music started, and she danced beautifully!

When she finished she bowed and the audience cheered. Bella glanced over at Miss Patti in the wings—she was smiling and clapping too.

Bella was very proud when the audience and Miss Patti clapped for her.

On the way home from the theater Bella sat in the backseat and smiled as she closed her eyes. Even though she is fluffier than the other bunnies, she felt strong and beautiful. After all, Bella is perfect just the way she is.

About the Author

Nina Koch has been dancing her entire life. She owns two dance studios in California. The busy mother of three believes that everyone should feel fabulous in their own skin (or fur) whether they're short, tall, thin, or fluffy.

Bella Bunny is Nina Koch's first children's book.